Words

=

Power

By Michael T. Roberson

I dedicate this book to my son who one day I hope will look back at this, and take something positive away from it. Thank you for letting me steal time away from you to write. I appreciate the support I've gotten during this journey; my family, friends, & coworkers all pushing me to make the transition from writer to author. I truly can't thank you all enough. This is only the beginning!!!

Words

=

Power

WORDS are a form of communication used to communicate our thoughts, & feelings; used to express ourselves. We use this practice of communication daily to help us touch the ones around us, and impact our lives. Simple yet advanced, there were various writing systems & 1000's of different languages created between us over time! Just as our skill with them has grown, so has our use of them. The times have proven how great their impact can be! With much passion many have learned to use them to inspire; to influence loved ones, communities, even nations. Many more have used them with the cruelest intentions. In countless ways words have aided some of the world's most inspirational leaders, & vilest individuals in requiring whatever they desired. Words are the good, the bad, but most importantly the great equalizer.

WORDS = POWER & this power I admire.

With this power...I can heal you. I can make you believe. I can hurt you. I can trick & deceive. I can persuade you. I can sell you a dream. I can teach you. Yes, there is much I can achieve, however what I choose to do is build...worlds. I will paint pictures within your mind, as you enter mines. I hope to connect with your heart & soul, and even capture your emotions. I will allow you to observe the merge of my craft & my vision. I will demonstrate my passion for storytelling. I will show you my creativity. With it I will make you acknowledge me!! To the ones who have known me I'd like to display how much I've grown. To the ones just getting to know me...

My name is Michael T. Roberson &...
These words of mine have power...

Table of Contents

"Mannn, those were the days!!!"

Our soul sings the melody. We reminisce on its jubilance & innocents plenty as our body reaches its ceiling. It exists as a common remedy for many. Valued memories forever reflected upon. A timeless treasure concealed within as time moves on. When we had it we were too young to fully appreciate its freedom. Little kings & queens with no worries or responsibilities; just laughter sailing into air as our fresh minds absorbed the world's offerings. We hold on to its grandest moments feeling as if nothing will measure up to them. Maturing, we even forget about its tiny setbacks for they can't compare to the hardships that follow. That being said even the stress of today sometimes have me missing its play, from hide & go seek, sports, and it tag, to the Saturday cartoons, sleepovers, and 'crushes' I had. You often heard, "Enjoy it while it lasts!" Then one day you find yourself conversing with friends, and somehow or someway you start saying things like "Remember when we used to..." or "Remember that time when..."

CHILDHOOD...

If you could...would you do it all over again? What moments would you relive? Would you let your eyes explore the same places, or meet the same faces? I tell myself I wouldn't change a thing, but to relive them I couldn't; recognizing in the end the only thing I'd be doing is creating the same memories. Great as they may be if there's any cons attached to this youth it's the fact that it's short lived, and within it there is so much more that hasn't been explored then has been. So the only thing left to do is be grateful that I reached its peak okay as I move forward to add finer memories to the gallery. My treasure is golden. It's a huge chapter in the story of life; from the people part of it to the lessons learned within. All of it played an important role in making me who I am today. That I am proud to say! However as my body ages day to day every so often I pop open that treasure chest & say... "Mannn, those were the days!!!"

(A Piece written by Michael T. Roberson)

Broken Dreams

A dream is hope, a wish in reality. Our sleep reflects them & we live to attain them!

Strength, love, loyalty & devotion were the moral pillars that raised one woman high. A marriage & kids with the one she loved was the dream she realized. However on this day the five days a week secretary, sat at work lugging a lonesome soul. There her thoughts & feelings flustered her, and her emotions quickly became too difficult to control. She rushed into the restroom to hide the showing of her distress. Placing her cluttered purse on the sink; into the mirror she stared asking herself 'Why?' Her make-up & eye liner ruined from the trail of tears left on her face. Reflecting on what could've been; gleeful images she hoped would soon come true were left shattered.

Her love damaged by her lover. Her dream stolen by another. She was several weeks removed from finding out that he was expecting a child from another woman! Her reality had become an unescapable nightmare. Wishing the busy demand of work would help subside the haunting thought; yet from the miserable appearance that gazed back at her it seemed as if the situation was starting to be unbearable.

She knew deep down however the only thing she could do is bear. Her hand snagged a paper towel hanging from the roll. She teased it with a dab of water, and began to wipe her face as she had done plenty of times since it all began. More eye liner & make-up she applied around her red, glossy eyes. Adding the final touches she practiced a smile in the mirror. Even though she pretended & presented it well; it hurt to do so knowing there was no truth behind it. Onward she went anyway heading back to her desk with a new face aiming to get through the remaining hours of her shift.

'What next??' The simple question was a difficult one to answer; and one she had pondered about while leaving work. Staying with concerned family the scarred woman refused to go back to the place she shared with him......the place she called home for three years. She stood outside of the sky reaching building; hesitation within her mind &bones. Unsure of the future waiting ahead thoughts heavily weighed on her mind. Yet they were so distracting nonetheless her feet released from her stationary stance. Through the busy streets &sidewalks of rush hour her feet guided her across town; her mind too intoxicated with thought to care where she was going.

During her walk the familiar noise of her phone vibrating inside of her purse stopped her. Digging for it, her eyes locked on the screen. It was him. Not able to even stomach his voice she ignored it. Every emotion that recently visited her cycled through her again as the phone in her hand vibrated. She could feel her eyes watering before it had stopped. The shadow of a gliding cloud struck her while she stood recovering from the moment. Paralyzed, people around her stared at her with worry. Soon enough however she could feel her flesh heat up when the warming sun found her again.

She broke her trance looking for her next move. A lengthy breeze slapped her lifting her hair. That's when she noticed the branches of full trees waving at her from a city park across the street. They lured her across the four lane road full of traffic, and into the park's world.

A cement path guided her. Its realm was beautiful; full of life & activity. Flowers of all colors were planted at the trunk of the trees that invited her inside. The sound of small birds caught her ear. Squirrels darted over the trimmed short, pure green grass. Paired jogging partners greeted her with smiles as they went pacing past her. Farther inside there were more people, busy clutching onto the leashes of small dogs. One individual enjoyed a nice read on one of the many benches on the path, and a couple picnicked yards away. The woman felt surrounded by 'PEACE' & 'HAPPINESS'; a feeling that had been missing from her life for what had seemed like forever. It all had nearly pulled a grin out of her.

The stroll continued, and with every step she could feel her character resurfacing; slowly climbing from the shallow pit it had been secluded in. Then while absorbing its sights a tune crept into her body. It helped lift her spirit even higher as she sought out where it came from. It wasn't long before she found out. Near the park's small pond the melody of a guitar showered nature from the lap of one soul on the horizon of the grass. Lovely it was, its soft strings streaming into each other as its rhythm struck her heart. This was exactly what she needed! Finding a nearby bench she sat &accepted the peace of mind it offered staring away into the pond's gleam.

However she was soon reminded this peace that consumed her was only a temporary fix. As she had begun to make herself comfortable the gentleman who was playing his guitar had abruptly stopped. She looked back at him as he rose from his place on the blades. The guitar went inside its case, the strap went over his shoulder, and the man was gone. There she remained on the bench afterwards dreading the return to her reality. However it could not be helped. The pain of her broken dream was too great, so out of the park she went, back to continue enduring it!

Broken Dreams part 2

Earlier that day one man relaxed his drained body on the stoop of his porch. Several years early of thirty, he was two hours removed from another overnight shift, and two dollars removed from minimum wage. It seemed as if shut-off notices had come to his house more frequently than pay checks these days, he thought to himself as he went through mail just left by the mail man. Despite hard times his mind was able to sail away; thinking of a life where he could support himself doing what he loved to do the most. He looked at the guitar shaped case that rested beside him. However looking at it brought a stir of mixed feelings. It embodied disappointment & failure to him yet it was the one piece of his life that gave him jubilance. He rose, and hoisted it over his shoulder. After the mail was placed inside the house he then locked up, his tired legs carried him away from his home. He could feel the day's sun had just begun to heat the city's streets rather early, yet his mind was busy thinking of the trialing history with his five string instrument.

Since he first discovered how much he loved to play his heart & guitar have been in sync with each other. Yearly he honed his skill, and it didn't take long before his mind salivated over the thought of being able to make it his livelihood. Early on he schooled to learn more about his craft, and while doing so he determinately entered a few local talent competitions. Large money prizes went to the winners, but disappointedly he had never finished as one. Then in time school became a dilemma. After his second year it became too much to afford, and he was forced to quit. Holding on to a dead end job, doubts started to creep into his mind as his failures mounted & the unsuccessful road became lengthy.

Then his road came upon happiness with a local band! They played at bars, diners, & events all over; even travelling some. The part he loved the most was when he'd do his solo. No one else singing or playing; just him & the guitar pouring out the vibe in his heart as he captured the crowd. A smile peeked from his face as he replayed the image of audiences cheering after his performance. That was one of the few great memories he would never let go.

An unfortunate event caused him to part ways with the band however. Sadly a highway collision claimed his father, and left his mother critically injured. Looking after his mother he struggled with its emotional toll, and for a long time became withdrawn from the world around him. A dream left unreached. No longer able to see it; his vision has been blurred. Since, his recovery has been a slow one, but through it all the one thing that he never peered away from was his guitar. The sound of those strings still remained to be his solace. It wasn't his living, but it was a way to escape the reality he lived in.

In little time he arrived at the stoop of another home, relieved to leave the sun's vision as he walked under the porch roof. He opened the screen door to knock, and twice he did before the front door opened. On the other side was the woman who he had loved dearly, and now comforted as she had done him......his mother. The light wrinkles on her face peaked as her grin stretched. He entered leaving the guitar at the door against the wall, and they did what they'd done at least twice a week; gave each other good company. They talked, laughed, and shared each other's life for a while; it being a brief liberation from the stressing thought & difficult absence of their loved one. The bond they forged helped fight the loneness. Aiding each other, after the life changing car accident, it was something they both profoundly valued.

Without realizing nearly half the day escaped. That was no surprise to them. It happened quite often when the two got together. In a great mood thanks to the visit, he figured he'd leave wanting to relish the remainder of the day before another late shift. Announcing his departure he went to collect his guitar, stepped outside the comfort of his mother's air conditioned home, and gave her a hug before going. In great spirit he paced on. Outside, the sun had never let up and it was too early for it to do so now.

Knowing he wasn't yet ready to retreat back home, the spirited walk ended at a park. Its beauty visually matched his soulful aura. It was only fitting to relax himself there, and in the shadow of a tree he did so. The guitar case was opened, and the polished instrument was pulled out from it. He gently held it like a mother holding her newborn! A struggling man with a gift in his hands, he ran his fingers across all the strings, and began to deliver his soul through tune. Passing by, people could feel the glee behind the ear friendly sound. With claps going & smiles showing in little time he had attracted a pleasant group of park visitors. He returned his grin to the small impressed audience. As time moved the shade he sat in moved, old faces progressed on, new ones took their place, and the talented man stayed in the moment. It reminded him of his time with the band. He didn't want it to stop! Unfortunately his fingers became worn, so giving in to their cry he eventually confessed to the tiny gathering.

The animated group gave him one more round of applause. Then the man watched as everyone slowly left to continue on with their day. Uplifting it was. Once he was alone again his head went to the grass. His pupils gazed into the branches above, and for some time he daydreamed as his fingers relaxed. "One more" he thought. The love for his craft wouldn't let him stop until he played one last tune. Back into position his body went, closing his eyes he started his melody, and he would make sure his last would be his best. Sadly however there was no group to appreciate it. Feeling wonderful when he finished, he put his instrument back into its case to head home; not noticing there was a stranger listening who had appreciated his sound more than any stranger he had met that day.

~To be continued~

Building Houses

One woman... One man... It began...

    It began with a feeling. A priceless feeling not even the wealthiest could buy. This feeling God himself respected, choosing not to control nor would he try. Ironic being that it felt like a gift that could only come from the heavens above. Their spirits vivid & veins circulating love. Their hearts began to beat for each other. Two young souls blessed with a growing affection for one another. The twinkle in their pupils spoke of pleasure. Their lover's flesh they smothered. Time spent together they wanted forever.

    The youthful passion seeming everlasting; ever did they stop to think maybe they were moving too fast! Fast?!? Love knows no speed, no control, no limits, and so together they accelerated. On the path to forever a home was being created. Their affection molding & lifting each other; flying like the flight of feathers. They travelled the uncharted together. To these young minds this was rare. No other happiness could compare....to the happiness they shared.

    To devote yourself eternally is an act upon great stimulation, but through its period comes tribulations; situations that invite confrontations. The framed picture they created would soon crack from the hardships of reality. To this love time which was then friendly would soon feel like an enemy. They would begin to lose direction. Just like many before them they began to fall to their imperfections.

    Characters change. Inevitable wrongdoings & mistakes cause pain. Maybe it's the selfishness of greed; or the lure of lust we desire to feed. Their sins hide. Trust struggles to survive as honesty turns to lies. The mirror shows the calm, but inside their souls cry. Misunderstood emotions soon rise. Apologies are thrown over the wounds. Yet the scars left behind are bone deep, and to forget would be too soon. It's difficult for the remembrance of hurt to leave the mind, so the search for true forgiveness becomes hard to find.

The hurt has been dealt. The love for each other fades behind the love for one's self. All of this steers one to isolation. They now have their blueprint, and have built their foundation. Within the heart the pain was engraved. For every hurtful blow a new layer was paved. Higher & higher their walls became, and before they realized two new houses were made.

Two more homes stood tall as the one they shared crumbled. These homes built desperately to find comfort through the struggle. Restricted from feeling the glee they shared by the homes within; afraid to let any more pain seep inside to capture them. The sacrifice of solitude for protection seemed to be the answer, however even within their protective walls the problem was a cancer. It slowly ate away at their core. The pain already inside consumed them more. It was clear the house the two built within was just a symbol of them being scorned.

Not able to escape the ache. They began to think maybe the house they built within their flesh was a mistake. Longing for the happiness they once knew through the window they peeked. Distant in a shared world each other's eyes they now seek. Their hand grasping for hope when they looked down it was the door knob in reach. Gazing cautiously, their lover's pupils they could read. Let's work this out. Reopen the door to your heart, and let me in. Hold my hand. Let the demolition begin.......

(A PIECE WRITTEN BY MICHAEL T. ROBERSON)

Mother's Will...
"Where there's a will there's a way."

I'm here...
So faint, so tiny, that I question my own existence.
This racing, thumping feel within me is real however. I cannot
question that. I may not understand how, but I've come to
realize I am real too. So here I am comfy & waiting...warmth
all around me with this sense that I belong here.

This overcasting voice I can hear through my
undeveloped ears. The slight vibration of it tingles me. It's
pleasant & welcoming to my soul. Its soft spoken tone spoke
with laughter & freedom.

As I begin to settle in my home my presence is soon
recognized. A rush of emotions enters from the walls around
me, yet what's raiding isn't inviting. Shock & denial are the
first. The reality of me isn't easy to comprehend. Then worry
& fear followed. All of them flooded my home but why? Why
this reaction...these emotions? Is there something wrong with
me? I feel fine. My heart remains beating. My body still
grows. I don't understand. What's the matter?

I must observe to learn, and in time I do. A new &
relevant voice soon presented itself, deep, strong & aggressive.
This voice clashed against the soft one I've grown to love.
Unfriendly the words were back & forth. In discussion of me

the deep voice unhappily aimed harsh words that could pierce my fragile body. The other protected me however, carrying & fighting behind its beliefs & morale.

When the argument was over however, I could feel the weeping of the wounded soul. Sad it was, and to feel it made it even worse. Alone, lost, & confused it felt with so many "Whys" it asked. Even though I was there, there was nothing I could do to help! My voice could not yet be heard. My touch could not yet be felt, so I was forced to feel the pain & hurt for what had seemed like forever.

......Wait more voices, unfamiliar & fresh!! Their words, and the feel they generated were just the same. Feelings I hadn't yet experience. Kind & refreshing, these voices rescued us from our solitude. I could feel their support. This love that was being passed around from one soul to the next unconditionally, and though I didn't know them nor did they know me they cared for I...for me!! Their compassionate love showered me.

With them around, it gave my protector the strength to push forward, as optimistic & loving as ever. The nourishment I had begun to receive was amazing...perfect! Of course I was aware there was plenty of the unknown on the outside to absorb, but my curiosity along with my anxiousness to do so became dormant. I didn't want to be anywhere else. Grateful I was feeding off the happiness between us.

Time braced our bond, and it became everything to me. Nothing could break it!! There was still one determined to do so however. Another argument soon commenced with the unforgettable intimidating threat, and once again my existence was challenged. This time however my guardian's approach was different. My protector's will was at its highest displaying confidence that surprised the other. Doing their ride of sensitive differences questions galloped through me. Why couldn't this one accept me? This life I was given…is it not as valuable as theirs? How could one cherish me and the other want nothing to do with me…want to end me? I wanted badly to understand, but all of the circumstances were still unclear to me.

In the midst of my own wonders the conflicting intensity had quickly risen. In yelling tone they cracked each other's spirits aiming for each other's weaknesses. This was something very familiar to my guardian & me, so in response my protector's defense strengthened. The other however did not respond very well. At the peak of it all a violent nudge came from the now broken & frustrated one suddenly shaking my place of resting. While absorbing its surprise the gravity shifted. All of the one that carried me quickly felt above me! Then a shouting whine of agony exhaled from my protector as my home's heaviness collapsed on top of me. The incoming walls underneath & around me struck my delicate body with velocity & force.

Damaged I laid in stillness, listening to silence. The sore & sensitive bruising throbbed like my heart; however unlike it the feel was unkind to my body. As weak & faint as ever I was in a fight to hang on to everything I knew. Struggling to do so my guardian's sound was absent to aid me…to comfort me. I yearned to hear it. With much relief the other voice was gone as well. Instead others quickly replaced it with much concern. The care giving to us was extreme, and while we healed they monitored us.

Then finally my inspiring carrier returned with a feeble tone. Speaking directly to me the saddened voice tried desperately to encourage me, strengthening & motivating my recovery. Many times however worry & fear revisited. The situation took its toll on the tired soul, but together we fought through thinking only of each other. Often during our lengthy battle even the close caring & lovely bundle of souls I had begun to recognize established their support within us. With reassurance my recovery became a jubilant growth.

Before long a building eagerness had grown wildly. I wasn't yet sure why, but I couldn't help but to feel the same way! The feeling ran through me. It was a time of importance & anticipation. Then one expressed "It's a boy!!" soon enough. Tears rained from above, and a soft touch came from the other side! Rubbing my home with tenderness the moment's happiness was unforgettable......amazing!! My development excited even myself.

As I was beginning to outgrow my home the joy never ceased. It only spread. Every voice around was now welcoming me. It made me wonder about "that" other voice however. Despite the threat it presented I wondered about it. Whatever happened to it...to its presence? Nothing to give me my answer I freed myself of the thought. With only the positives molding me I wanted to let my guardian feel my appreciation, so I reached for the wall in front of me. There my hand searched, and then my guardian's met mines. Almost unreal the moment was. It was the first time we were able to connect on this level; a yearning physical connection. Through the wall we could feel each other's fleshly, circuiting warmth.

Over time my growth made it easier for us to connect. We got used to playing with one other. It made me anxious once again about getting to the other side. I wanted to play without the interference of the closing walls around me. Time became my foe. My mind was ready to leave yet my body was not; so with my development slowly reaching its peak inside of this shrinking home patience had become my friend. Waiting for that golden moment when we finally meet each other.

"William!!!" My guardian said I would be named. I like it, and fitting to its meaning I vow to protect you as you have protected me! To take care of you as you have me! To love you as you have loved me! With openness I will even try to understand the reason why I was never accepted in one's eyes, and others to come. This journey here has shown me much, but I know there is much more on the other side; much more happiness, much more hurt, and everything in between. That's why I'm thankful for the fight you installed into me.

Now I feel I'm ready to depart from my home!
I am ready to see you; those bold eyes, and free smile!
I am ready to see them!
I am ready to see the world!
I am ready to live!
I am...

Mother's Will!!!
(A PIECE WRITTEN BY MICHAEL T. ROBERSON)

Broken Dreams part 3

A dream breaks, and at that moment the only thing you can do is watch as the shattered pieces fall around you. Like broken glass it surrounds you, and in the reflection of every piece lays the images of your failed dream. It mocks & scorns you emotionally, spiritually, mentally, & even physically. Whether you pick up those pieces in an effort to put them together, or you choose to walk away from it all, the pain will be unavoidable. You are forced to deal with it, hoping it doesn't define you, or defeat you.

For the woman it was clear the short, yet healing period she spent at the park 'that day' countered her pain.........but only momentarily. Her world quickly returned to misery, and was shrouded with it! No matter where she was, work, familiar neighborhoods, stores & restaurants, with family & friends; the scattered pieces around her broken dream remained. They were all elements that were there prior to her love's betrayal & haunted her after. Every day, something, someone, or someplace reminded her of some fond memory before her lover's unfaithfulness. It killed her inside.

Staying at her parent's house in the room she once called her own; she happened to be up early from a sleepless night. Thoughts of her situation tormented her, as she laid in bed. This was nothing new for her. The reality of her dream had her dealing with nightmares every other night, but thankfully an off day from work was ahead of her. She stared at the morning sun, lit wall which was spread with several older photos of her younger years upon it. The one thing she couldn't help but notice in all the photos was her smile. It was a symbol of her happiness, and she yearned for it back. The woman was so lost in thought she was numb to the tears her pillow absorbed. Light quickly overthrew the room, capturing her busy mind. She rose from her position to sit on the edge of the bed; sure that lying there any longer would only hurt her. Opened & unorganized suit cases filled with her clothes & belongings were piled in the corner of the room. She went through them searching for comfortable clothing to match the day's weather.

The morning got older & the now dressed woman was desperate to escape the war her mind & spirit had been battling. In the kitchen she stared out the window in wait of the kettle on the stove to whistle, and minutes away from a hot coffee. Beyond the glass a river of clouds challenged the sun's reign. People & vehicles went by. Life outside was moving she observed, however the silence inside let her tired mind speak. She could hear it asking for a break from the heart aching, & reminiscing. What to do? Who to spend this time with…..this misery with? She pondered with uncertainty. Then, just as a slight toot crept into her ears, she was fed a nice thought; a great way to hopefully answer her plea.

There the woman was, gazing down the park's outer realm once again. With optimism she had returned. The recent memory & feeling of her first visit she aspired to duplicate. The thick trees waved at her reappearance, inviting her again to come inside. Despite the cloudy & breezy day she wasted no time entering with a wishful pace. Retracing her steps through the park she observed its life. There were a few people in suits chatting as they walked pasted her. One of the men aggressively gawked her down, and she could feel his heavy stare. Uncomfortable, she tried not to look back, and couldn't wait to escape their view. A small group then came zooming past her on bikes. Afterwards she quickly noticed she was still seeking the happiness of her first visit, however just like the amazing luster of 'that day' it failed to compare to her first visit.

Appreciative nonetheless the young woman continued on; soon sitting on one of the benches. Her hair sailed the wind as she relaxed. The slight thought of her on the bench last visit had suddenly come to mind. The sun was much brighter then, and the park was much livelier. Her eyes closed, and she could even recall the tune blessing the air that day; that guitar! Nearly able to hear it, more images from her first visit revisited her mind as she hoped to recapture that glee. Bringing back the small collection of feel good moments were beginning to work. Her mind & spirit were on an adventure.

Only grounded by her flesh, her eye lids remained stretched over her pupils as happiness refilled her. Abruptly however a sensation of something wet struck her. Splash.....then another & another. The venture ended, and her pupils drifted open to the world again. She instantly noticed how dim the world around her became. The river of clouds had brought in grey skies. A light drizzle had begun to sprinkle the park. She observed the people around her hurrying to their destinations, as she reluctantly accepted the light shower. The woman wasn't yet ready to leave, but as the pour got heavier she felt as if she was being pushed from the joy of her day. Upset, she stood. Then in composed fashion she walked toward the nearest exit of the park.

With her clothes & hair collecting water, and rain slapping her in the face, she walked the wet path. Soon she was able to see the exit, but quickly she paused after a familiar tune found her through the thickening rain. Her eyes searched to find the faint sound's source. Following her ears however, she found actually who she imagined it would be; the same man playing the same guitar she remembered from her last visit. Under a small wooden gazebo he focused on his guitar. Soaked, the woman approached him. With every step the harmony of his music doused her soul again with joy. Finally reaching the gazebo she gazed with relief; happy that she didn't have to return to her dark world.

For the man hoisting the guitar had hope to duplicate his memorizing visit as well, but thanks to the weather he played alone. No group of smiles surrounded him, no claps to be heard; however he didn't let that demoralize his playing. Protected from the rain fall, its mist sprayed him. He zoned in on his moist, fiddling fingers practicing on the guitar. Soon enough the gentleman looked up to gaze upon the pour around him. Yet waiting for his eyes was a drenched woman gazing upon him.

Surprised he nearly fumbled his guitar to greet her. She smiled, and complimented him on his talent. He was appreciative of her kindness, but felt even more grateful when he was quickly asked to play again. Without hesitation he continued on to please her. He watched her eyes enjoyably study how he created the charming sound of his next tune. Ending it all too soon however he was pushed to follow up with another. With a heavy rain surrounding them he felt as if they were blocked from the world, and looking at this woman who had found him; her desperate grace & want for his sound made him feel as if he was meant to be there with her. He was unsure of the purpose he served, but he played on. One after another he introduced her to lovely melodies. Her responding expressions fed him. Within the rain his connection with her grew beyond the connection of any face he had met his prior visit.

Two dreams broken by circumstances, neither of them knew how they were aiding each other through their personal storm within. In time the rain slowed & stopped just as he had finished his fourth. Relaxing his fingers afterwards he looked around, at the park's dripping trees, & puddle full pathways. Joining him, the woman didn't bother to ask him to play another one. Her solace was high enough. Their smiling eyes found each other. At that moment in both of their minds they knew they were done there, however before their departure the woman insisted on seeing him soon. He offered tomorrow, wanting badly to display more of his skill.

"Who was this woman?" He asked himself showing up to the park in the late afternoon the next day. The breeze had returned from yesterday as well giving him a slight chill, but there he waited. The woman arrived shortly. She had just left a long work shift behind, and was pleased to see him. Another remarkable session quickly came about that day, and every day for nearly an entire week; little by little he had gotten this woman. Such a unique relationship they had built at this park sharing their life with one another. Each day he came to the park with a different set of tunes from his long list to play for her. Others of course were drawn to his sound as well, but he found himself only playing to please her. Surrounding applauds & smiles given to him were suddenly invisible. Within their time together she even grew to challenge him, but he didn't realize how much until he had ran out of different melodies to introduce. That's when a special idea crossed his mind.

He admitted to the woman his list had been played through. However, he told her he wouldn't be back for another week, and when he returned he would have an afternoon full of new material. New tunes dedicated & made especially for her. She was enthusiastic about his words. Farewells followed, and they both looked forward to the next time they would see each other.

The days before them however, would be struggling ones until then. For the woman would have no outlet; no escape for the heartbroken soul. Reminded daily in some way of the dream turned nightmare she would even revisit the park hoping to free her spirit of negative feelings, and wishing maybe to come across the gifted man. She knew she wouldn't see him, yet as the days would accumulate thoughts of 'that man' & his talent would gratefully replace the thoughts of her broken dream. She was happy to let them; realizing even the man's absence would then become helpful to her spirit.

For the man would once again have a goal in front of him; a task to overcome. He had stopped pushing himself some time ago, but the presence of his woman had rejuvenated him. Entering the days with a fresh energy, his after work mornings were occupied with breakfast, reading & studying music; afternoons consisted of porch relaxation & practicing tune combinations uncommon to his ear. With every new idea coming from his instrument he'd try to visualize the woman expressions.

Then when that day finally came they both entered the magnificent realm of the park. From different entrances they walked their path towards the center in search of each other's faces. Plenty of faces filled the park, but near the gazebo their eyes finally connected once again. With an outer reserve she anxiously gazed at him & his guitar, not knowing her dream would soon exist within him! She would fall in love all over again with him, what he represented to her, his trialing spirit & the beauty that came from it! Nor did he know how immense her role would be in his dream, or how she would become his biggest fan & supporter; motivating new melodies! How she would drive him & his talent to new heights! How he would go on to amaze crowds & conquer stages! The man waved breaking the stare between them, so she waved back matching his grin. Their legs would soon close the small distance between them, & so would the distance between their dreams......

Dreams are blessings; even the broken ones. There's meaning & value behind them all!

(A PIECE WRITTEN BY MICHAEL T. ROBERSON)

The Effect...

'The Effect' is happening many places, every day, in countless different ways.
It may have already happened to you, but if not…just wait.
Take a glimpse inside & understand it.
Here lies 'The Effect……'

An older lady lies across a hospital bed; her wrinkled body clinging onto warmth as thick blankets smothered her. With medicines & I.V.'s entering her fragile frame she's aware her last days are upon her. A woeful battle with cancer has defeated her flesh, however her soul remains unbroken. As the light of morning greeted her face she stared at the tearful eyes of her visiting family; her son & two daughters. She relished having them there. Her five grandchildren stood at their side, all but one looking at her with a clueless gaze. The oldest grandchild, a young boy could sense something was wrong, and as the lady stared back at him she understood what she had to do. It was time to say her final goodbyes to the grandchildren. A quick thought on it hurt the lady dearly, but she refused to show it. Instead she encouraged them to come closer. They came, and she took her time wrapping her arms around every one of them for the last time; kissing them for the last time. Saving the oldest for last she spoke to him……

"This may be the last time we see each other for a while, but I want you to remember my love. I will always be with you. I will always be watching you, and I know you will make me proud."

Across town one man stared nervously into his large mirror mounted onto his bedroom wall. He fixed, & adjusted the tie around his neck before laying his collar down. His long sleeved, button-up shirt was tucked into his pressed slacks. His clothes fit him nicely, and with his dress shoes to match he appeared to be ready for his interview. The changes that would come if given the job, he could nearly visualize them. He practiced his introduction in the mirror, sticking his hand out to give his reflection a firm handshake. Yet, he could not shake off his nervousness. He rehearsed his words trying to cover his anxiety with preparation. Then he followed with a tiny prayer before leaving. Soon, he was shaking the manager's hand, and with professionalism & passion he sold himself aiming for his dream. Ten minutes later the manager stood from his chair, and aimed to shake his hand once again......

"Impressive! I would like to be the first to welcome you onboard."

Another gentleman that evening was feeling a different type of nervousness as dusk filled the sky. Tonight was the night! A large dinner party with family & friends was waiting for him & his significant other. He knew this would be a night neither of them would forget. With four words, one question he could have his woman forever. He thought upon it uncontrollably. Both he & his woman were fairly young, and they had only been together for a little over a year. However his love was beyond the clouds. He could envision himself waking up to her for the rest of his years, and he felt his love for her could conquer any difficult situation they would meet along the way. The moment had quickly arrived, and the seconds had begun to slow. He looked at their circle of loved ones at the table, his heart racing through his chest. A light sweat had built on his face. Then he looked into her lovely eyes, and knelt before her divine physique......

"Will you marry me?"

As the woman absorbed her moment with glossy eyes staring down at her bold, future husband; another young girl could only hope to dream that far. From the six-floor balcony of the high rise she lived in, her tears fell to the earth below. Sadly it wasn't the first time she found herself there questioning her very existence. Since she can remember she's felt this way. Branded a "mistake" by her resenting mother the young girl found it hard to bear her young years. Then constantly labeled "fat" & "stupid" by fellow classmates; her beautiful soul has gone unrecognized by the blind world around her. Daily she is tormented with verbal assault to the point she believes every word, and the beauty of her soul even goes unrecognized by herself. Damaged, she cries. This young adolescent wants desperately to escape her pain so she contemplates jumping. No one is there to hear her cry, to save her, or to feed her wounded soul WORDS of healing. Instead the foul names & treatment she's dealt with her whole life hurtfully replays through her skull. "No more...no more." she tells herself as she climbs over the edge ready to follow her tears.

THE EFFECT......

These individuals only connection is 'The Effect', but do you understand it? It's power? The effect of moments riding emotions, guided by WORDS. WORDS that have the power to change your life, to mold it, or damage it. WORDS you may never let go. Whether you're the little boy who has been lifted by his grandmother's final words, the young girl who's been tormented by them, or anyone in between; I believe we all are destined to one day be captured by 'The Effect'! The intriguing unknown is what role will it play in your life?!?

(A PIECE WRITTEN BY MICHAEL T. ROBERSON)

Students of Life

I believe we are all Students of Life. We observe the lives around us, learning as we search for our own meaning during our time here. That search can become a complicated one, & the world shows no compassion never stopping or slowing down for no one. As people we skirmish to keep up with its pace. We are born with our personal stages of life set; lurking.....& waiting for our arrival. These stages in our life can become so difficult that our meaning to this world soon becomes lost as we scarcely manage to make it through the harsh chapters of life.

Each path as different as the person that's walking it; while you're absorbing life's embracing ups and strenuous downs there will be tough choices to make, & feelings we must understand. As a "Student of Life" we must realize that these circumstances, these struggles are just the natural order of life. Life without struggle then isn't life......its heaven right? With that being said all we can do is strive to overcome the cold chapters of tribulations hoping not to lose our way. With growth we learn, and with faith we endure!

I thank you for reading!

This Student of Life is a believer in God, and I thank him for this outlet I have been given to exercise my mind. I have a passion for writing, and the creativity & different challenges it presents. Writing is an art, so every moment that I write I make an intuitive effort to become a better artist. I enjoyed doing this project, and I hope even more so you enjoyed reading it. Being able to share this with you is rewarding to say the least. Until next time……

FINAL WORDS

"**WORDS = POWER**, & this power I admire. How will you utilize this power?" **–Michael T. Roberson**

"Cherish your visions, and your dreams as they are the children of your soul, the blueprints of your ultimate achievements." **-Napoleon Hill**

"Believe you can and you're halfway there." **-Theodore Roosevelt**

"Things may come to those who wait, but only the things left by those who hustle." **–Abraham Lincoln**

"Put your heart, mind, and soul into even your smallest acts. This is the secret of success."**-Swami Sivananda**

"Happiness is not something you postpone for the future; it is something you design for the present." **-Jim Rohn**

"Some people want it to happen, some wish it would happen, others make it happen." **–Michael Jordan**

"By failing to prepare, you are preparing to fail."**-Benjamin Franklin**

"Think twice before you speak, because your words and influence will plant the seed of either success or failure in the mind of another." **-Napoleon Hill**

"The ultimate measure of a man is not where he stands in moments of comfort and convenience, but where he stands at times of challenge and controversy." **–Martin Luther King, Jr.**

"If we did all the things we are capable of we would literally astound ourselves." **–Thomas A. Edison**

"Let me into your lives, your world. Live on me, so that you may become truly alive." **–Jesus Christ**